The Sidewalk Toy Stand

By Richard Kelso
Illustrated by Pat Paris

Copyright © 2000 Metropolitan Teaching and Learning Company.
Published by Metropolitan Teaching and Learning Company.
Printed in the United States of America.
All rights reserved. No part of this work may be reproduced, transmitted, or utilized in any form or by any means, electronic, mechanical, or otherwise, including photocopying and recording, or by any storage and retrieval system, without prior written permission from Metropolitan Teaching and Learning Company, 33 Irving Place, New York, NY 10003.

ISBN 1-58120-039-0

3 4 5 6 7 8 9 CL 03 02 01

"Look at this place. Look at all my old toys," said Dan. "I have to put them all away."

"I have old toys, too," said Nina. "There is no place for my new toys. I would like to get rid of my old stuff. I want to give it away."

"We can sell our old toys and books," said Sara. "Other boys and girls will want what we have. Mom said we can have a stand on the sidewalk. Carlos and Marta can sell there, too. I will ask them to come."

"First, we can fill the wagon with our stuff," said Sara. "Then, we can set up the stand."

"That is a good plan," said Dan. "We will make money. Then we can get new toys."

"Take this stuff out first," said Sara. "Carlos and Marta are filling up their wagon. I will go and get them."

"This wagon is stuffed," said Dan. "We have a lot to sell at our sidewalk stand."

"This stand looks good," said Dan. "It is filled with toys. When Carlos and Marta come we will have a lot more."

"Look. There is Carlos with his wagon," said Nina. "Marta and Sara are with him."

"We made it!" said Carlos. "We have a lot of stuff. We have toys, dolls, and books."

"Put your stuff on the stand," said Dan.

"Did you sell any toys yet?" asked Sara. "Did you make any money?"

"A boy gave me a dime for a toy," said Dan. "A girl was looking at a doll. But that was it."

"I hope we sell all the toys," said Carlos. "Then we can get new stuff."

"I plan to make a lot of money. I am going to get some new games," said Dan.

"I am going to go to the movies," said Marta.

"You are all adding up the money," said Sara. "But first, we have to sell some toys."

"No one wants my toys," said Nina. "I want to sell two dolls and my rabbit Fluff. Some girls came by, but no one wanted Fluff."

"I would like to have Fluff," said Marta. "But I have to make some money first."

"I like your doll Nell," said Nina. "We don't have any money, but we can trade. We can trade Fluff and Nell."

"I like your plan," said Marta. "I will have Fluff and you will have Nell."

"This book looks good," said Sara. "I want to get it, but I don't have any money."

"I would like to get some books, too," said Carlos. "We can trade books. Then we can get the books we want to read."

"I am selling all my good games," said Dan. "You like games, Marta. Get one."

"I am just looking," said Marta. "But I have my good games here, too. We can trade our games. What do you say to that?"

"Put all the new stuff in the wagon. The boys and girls who come by may want it," said Sara. "We can't sell it to them."

"What boys and girls?" asked Carlos. "Add it up, Sara. You and I have not made a dime!"

"So what?" said Sara. "We all got new stuff. It may be old, but it is new to us."

"I got Fluff," said Marta.

"I got little Nell," said Nina. "And we all had fun! It is all adding up to a good day."

"It is time to put our toys away," said Carlos.

"I just added up my money," said Dan. "I made a dime! One big dime!"

"Good for you," said Sara. "You can take the wagon back to our place."